BEAR -and- Bee

by Sergio Ruzzier

Disney • Hyperion Books
New York

To Giacomo and Pietro

Printed in Singapore • First Edition • 1 3 5 7 9 10 8 6 4 2 • F850-6835-5-12319
Designed by Whitney Manger
Text is set in Telegraph.
Art created in pen and ink on Arches paper with digital coloring.

Library of Congress Cataloging-in-Publication Data

Ruzzier, Sergio.
   Bear and Bee / by Sergio Ruzzier.—1st ed.
       p. cm.
   Summary: A hungry bear discovers that bees are not terrible monsters
who never share their honey.
   ISBN 978-1-4231-5957-5
   [1. Bears—Fiction. 2. Bees—Fiction. 3. Sharing—Fiction. 4. Prejudices—Fiction.] I. Title.
   PZ7.R9475Be 2013
   [E]—dc23   2011032426
                               Reinforced binding
                          Visit www.disneyhyperionbooks.com

"Mmm . . . Honey!"

"Would you like some honey?" says Bee.

"I would love some honey," says Bear.
"But what about the bee?"

"Have you ever seen a bee?" says Bee.

"No!" says Bear.
"I hope I never see a bee!"

"You are big," says Bee.
"Mm-hmm," says Bear.

"**You** have large teeth," says Bee.
"Uh-huh," says Bear.

"*You* have sharp claws," says Bee.
"Uh-oh," says Bear.

"I AM A BEE!"

"You are not a bee!" says Bee.
"You are a bear!"

"Oh, right," says Bear.
"I *am* a bear.
And what are you?"

"I am a bee!" says Bee.
"YOU are a bee?" says Bear.

"But you are not big,
and you don't have
large teeth,
and you don't have
sharp claws."

"Do you share your honey?"

"Would you like some honey?" says Bee.

"Wait for me!" says Bear.

"Mmm . . . Honey!"

"Bee, I am glad you are a bee."